ZAPATO POWER
FREDDIE RAMOS TAKES OFF

JACQUELINE JULES   art by MIGUEL BENÍTEZ

Library of Congress Cataloging-in-Publication Data

Jules, Jacqueline, 1956-
Zapato power : Freddie Ramos takes off / by Jacqueline Jules ; illustrated
by Miguel Benítez.
p. cm.
Summary: Freddie finds a mysterious package outside his apartment
containing sneakers that allow him to run faster than a train, and inspire
him to perform heroic deeds.
ISBN 978-0-8075-9480-3 (hc)
ISBN 978-0-8075-9479-7 (sc)
[1. Sneakers—Fiction. 2. Speed—Fiction. 3. Heroes—Fiction.]
I. Benítez, Miguel, ill. II. Title.
PZ7.J92947Zap 2010
[Fic]—dc22
2009025379

10 9 8 7 6 5 4 3 2 1 LB 14 13 12 11 10

The design is by Nick Tiemersma.

For more information about Albert Whitman & Company,
visit our web site at www.albertwhitman.com

ZAPATO POWER

FREDDIE RAMOS TAKES OFF

CONTENTS

1. A Box Changes My Life

A box changed my life. It was sitting outside Apartment 29G when I came home from Starwood Elementary.

My name, **FREDDIE RAMOS**, was written on it in big black letters. I'd never gotten a package like this.

"What did you get?" a deep voice asked.

I looked up to see Mr. Vaslov.
He had a paintbrush in his hand.
Mr. Vaslov takes care of Starwood
Park Apartments, and he is always
fixing something.

"I don't know yet," I said. "I can't open the box. It's taped up like a mummy."

"I'll look in my toolshed," Mr. Vaslov said. "I've got scissors there."

I followed him with my mummy box.

"Be careful," he said, as we walked. "The paint is still wet."

The toolshed looked bright, white, and all brand new. The last place Mom and I lived didn't have someone like Mr. Vaslov always trying to make things look nice. When big kids wrote bad words on the walls, the words stayed there a long time.

"Where did I put my scissors?" Mr. Vaslov said.

While Mr. Vaslov searched, I peeked in. I'd never seen inside the toolshed. There were tables and shelves full of wires, cables, batteries, and electronic stuff.

"Did you take apart a billion computers?" I asked.

"No," Mr. Vaslov laughed. "Only fifty."

Just as I was about to ask him why he was cutting up computers, Mr. Vaslov found his scissors.

We opened the box. First we saw lots of white packing popcorn.

Then we saw a sheet of purple paper. It had five words printed on it.

"'Zapato Power.'" Mr. Vaslov pushed his bushy gray hair away from his face. "That sounds interesting."

"Yeah." I turned the purple paper over. "Except I'm not sure what it means."

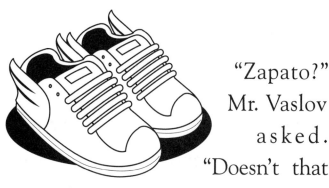

"Zapato?" Mr. Vaslov asked. "Doesn't that mean shoe in Spanish?"

"It sure does. But what kind of power is shoe power?"

I dug my hands back into the white packing. This time, I pulled out two purple sneakers with silver wings on the side.

"Exactly what I need! Uncle Jorge is the best!"

I figured it was Uncle Jorge in New York. No one else mailed me presents. I put down the sneakers and looked for a signed card in the packing popcorn.

"That's strange," I said. "Uncle Jorge always sends funny cards with his gifts."

Some of the popcorn spilled on the floor while I searched the box, but Mr. Vaslov didn't complain. Instead, he leaned down to pick up the purple sneakers.

"Nice!" he said. "A lot better than what you're wearing."

We both looked at my shoes. They were all torn up. Maria from next door said they looked like a dog chewed them. Mom promised to buy me new ones as soon as she paid this month's bills. Now Mom could use the money to buy something for herself. I had brand new purple sneakers with silver wings on the side!

2. I Race the Train

"Try them on," Mr. Vaslov suggested. "See if they fit."

The purple sneakers hugged my feet like they were made for me.

"Wow! They feel great!"

"All right, then," Mr. Vaslov said in that voice grownups use when they're tired of you and ready to go back to their own stuff. "Go try them out. The train should be coming by any second."

I stared at him. "Have you seen me racing the train?"

He grinned. "How could I miss it? You're out there by the track every afternoon."

It was true. After a long day at school, trying to sit still every time Mrs. Lane reminded me, I needed to let loose. And the train rumbled by on its overhead track, shouting, "Race Me! Race Me!" We were a mile from the station. When I heard the train coming, I spread my arms out, like an airplane taking off. Airplanes can beat trains. Of course it was just pretend, but racing made me run faster.

"Here it comes!" Mr. Vaslov smiled as the walls of the toolshed started to shake.

I waved a quick goodbye and headed out the door.

The purple sneakers made a soft buzzing sound. My feet felt light. I ran faster and faster until the grass was just a blur beneath me.

Smoke whooshed out of my heels. The wind whipped across my cheeks. My legs whirled so fast I could hardly see them.

But I could see the train. It was up there beside me, falling behind! And I was zooming ahead, like a supercharged engine in my purple sneakers. Rápido! My pretend game had turned real! I was as fast as an airplane, racing the train. And winning!

When I got to the station, I dropped to the ground behind the fence. The train roared in over me. I'd just run a whole mile in a few seconds!

Talk about Zapato Power! I looked down at my purple sneakers.

They were super shoes. I had super power! Where did Uncle Jorge get shoes like this? How fast could I get home to call him?

I stood up and spread out my arms.

ZOOM! ZOOM! Zapato!

My feet took off like jet wheels on a runway. One blink later, I was back at 29G.

3. The Mysteries Begin

"Gracias!" I shouted into the phone. "Thank you!"

"You're welcome," Uncle Jorge said. "What did I do?"

"You sent me Zapato Power! The fastest sneakers in the world!"

"Sneakers?" Uncle Jorge repeated. "Sorry. It wasn't me."

If Uncle Jorge hadn't sent me the shoes, who had?

"So what else is happening?" Uncle Jorge asked. "How's your head? You still keeping it short like a soldier?"

I laughed. Uncle Jorge always teased me about my hair. He said it made me look like my hero dad.

We talked a few minutes more. I told him about getting an *A* for the first time in spelling, and about the new basketball courts at school. Even though I'm shorter than most of the other guys, I can still get the ball through the hoop.

"Watch the mail," Uncle Jorge promised just before he said goodbye. "I'll get paid next week and send you something good."

"Thanks, Uncle Jorge." I hung up the phone, still wondering where my purple sneakers came from.

Maybe Mom could tell me. I always called to tell her I got home all right anyway. She worked in a busy doctors' office, answering telephones. I munched on pretzels while I waited on hold, listening to music and an electronic voice telling me my call was important.

"Did you leave a box on the

doorstep for me?" I asked when I finally got through.

"No, Freddie." Mom sounded puzzled. "I always leave things for you on the table."

I knew that was true, but when you're solving a mystery, you have to check everything out, even if it means saying mushy stuff to your mom on the phone.

"See you at six, mi hijito."

"Love you, too, Mom."

I'd made enough phone calls. It was time to investigate in other places.

I need to look at the box," I realized.

But it was still at Mr. Vaslov's shed. I fed my guinea pig, Claude the Second, and left 29G, wearing my new purple sneakers. They felt like foam under my feet.

"Mr. Vaslov!" I knocked on the toolshed door.

He opened it wearing safety goggles, like a scientist.

"I'm busy now, Freddie," he said. "Can I help you later?"

"I need the box my sneakers came in."

"Why do you want that?" Mr. Vaslov pushed his goggles up.

"I'm trying to find out who gave me my purple sneakers."

Mr. Vaslov scratched his face.

"Freddie," he said. "Just enjoy the sneakers. Don't worry about where they came from."

It was good advice, but I'm a curious guy.

"Please. Can you tell me where the box is?"

Mr. Vaslov pushed his goggles back down over his blue eyes.

"I put it out for the trash." He closed the door.

Luckily, the box was beside the smelly dumpster, not in it. My name and 29G, Starwood Park Apartments were written on the front in big black letters. There were lots of stamps on the box but no return address. I checked again for a card. Nothing.

All I knew was that the box came in the mail.

It wasn't much to go on.

What would my dad say about getting magic shoes in the mail?

Whenever I couldn't figure something out, I always tried to imagine what my father would tell me if he was around. It wasn't easy because I didn't have much time with him. He was off being a soldier most of my life. And then he wasn't there at all.

"Any luck with the box?" a voice above me asked.

I looked up to see Mr. Vaslov. He had a bag of garbage in his hand.

"No. It didn't tell me much of anything."

"Might as well give up, then," Mr. Vaslov said. "It's getting late."

I looked at my watch. Mom would be getting off the train soon. I thought about using my Zapato Power and running back to the station to surprise her. But then I thought about what I would say when Mom saw my new purple sneakers. I hadn't quite decided yet. What if she wouldn't let me keep them if I didn't know where they came from?

"I'd better go home," I told Mr. Vaslov. "Mom likes to see me doing my homework when she comes through the door."

4. A Pretty Regular Night for a Superhero

Ever since Mom finished her classes at the community college and got a better job, she's been big on school. I have to show her my papers, and we read chapter books together. I like reading at bedtime, but school didn't take up so much of my life when I didn't have to do my homework every night.

By the time I opened the door to 29G and gave a carrot treat to Claude the Second, it was 5:45. I took off my purple sneakers and put them under my bed. Mom wouldn't notice anything weird about me going around the house in socks. I figured I could tell her about the purple sneakers when she noticed them. Every once in a while, she looks under my bed, so the conversation would come up sooner or later.

Then I hurried to get my backpack open and my books on the table. But it was hard to concentrate on my homework. I kept thinking about running in my purple shoes, flying on the ground like a plane with giant wheels. Zapato Power! My whole life was about to change! And not in any of the ways Mom had promised when we moved into Starwood Park at the beginning of the school year. She had said we were going to spend more time together and my grades were going to get better. That stuff happened. But Mom hadn't predicted this. I had purple shoes that made me faster than a train. Was this my chance to become a hero like my dad?

"How about pizza for dinner?" Mom asked when she got home. "I'm too tired to cook."

"Pizza's fine with me." I jumped up and handed Mom the phone. We had the pizza number on speed dial. That was one of the best things about Mom having a better job. Good food for dinner wasn't a problem anymore.

While we waited for the delivery, Mom looked over my math problems and my spelling words.

"Your handwriting looks a lot neater, Freddie. I'm glad to see you're taking your time."

I was happy to see Mom smiling. She wasn't much of a smiler before we moved to Starwood Park. Her brown eyes always looked worried the way my friend Maria's did when we went to the street fair and rode the Ferris wheel. Maria is afraid of heights, and my mom is afraid of too many bills. She also worried a lot when I was little because Dad was a soldier.

I worried, too. The first time he went away, he came back just fine. The second time, he didn't. But everyone at his funeral called him a hero. That was two years ago.

I finished all my homework before dinner, so Mom and I had time to watch a couple of TV shows together after my bath. It was a pretty regular night. Not what you would expect for a guy that just got purple sneakers with super speed. What else can you do if your mom doesn't let you go out after dark?

At nine o'clock Mom and I got cozy on my bed and read another chapter of this book we got from the library. It's about this really smart kid who is kind of a superhero. He gives himself a cool fake name and uses the internet to keep a bully from bothering him. While we read, I kept thinking about my Zapato Power. Would it make me a superhero? Should I come up with a new name for myself—one that I could use when I did hero things? Mom kept reading, and my mind kept thinking bigger and bigger thoughts. Would I be able to make bullies stop picking on littler kids? Would I catch crooks and save people? And if I started doing stuff like that, would I need to tell my mom?

I almost went to sleep without

Mom finding out about the purple sneakers. She had her hand on the light switch when she remembered that I'd called her at work that afternoon.

"What was the box on the doorstep?" she asked.

It was time to confess. I leaned under my bed and pulled out the purple sneakers.

"Nice!" she said. "Did they come from Uncle Jorge?"

"No. I called him and asked."

Mom picked up the purple sneakers and traced the silver wings with her finger.

"I wonder if they came from one of your dad's friends."

"In the army?" I asked.

She nodded her head. "I talked to someone from his old unit last week. He asked about you. I remember telling him you were growing fast and wearing out your shoes. "

"That would have been nice of him to send me a gift. He doesn't know me."

"But he knew your dad," Mom said, giving me a kiss goodnight. "Sometimes, that's enough."

5. It's Not Easy to Be a Superhero at School

The next morning I went to school, ready to be a hero. I wanted to save a kid from a burning building or catch a criminal. Saving a cat would have been okay, too. But it's not that easy to be a hero when you go to elementary school. No one falls out of high windows. We don't even have a second story at Starwood Elementary. No one seems to need hero stuff. They need left-behind lunches and library books.

"My book is still in my desk!" Jason cried, as we turned the corner near the library.

"It's too late to go back for it now," Mrs. Lane, our teacher, said.

"But I can't get a new one if I don't give one back!" he wailed.

I was standing behind Jason at the end of the line.

This was the third time that day he'd cried. The first time was when he broke his favorite pencil. The second time was when Harold called him a crybaby.

"Why can't I go back?" Jason whined. "I'll be quick."

Jason wasn't fast about anything, except crying. But I was fast. The problem was getting caught. If a teacher sees you running in the halls, you're sent straight to the office. But could anyone see me running in my purple sneakers? Was I too fast to see? There was only one way to find out. I sped off around the corner.

Just my luck, Mr. Hadley, the assistant principal, was in the hall with Mrs. Connor, the principal. I took a chance and zoomed right past them.

"Did you hear a buzzing sound?" said Mr. Hadley.

"Just for a moment—with a wisp of smoke," I heard Mrs. Connor say.

I made it to our classroom, grabbed Jason's book, and got back in the library line before Jason finished wiping his eyes.

"My book!" he called. "How'd you get it?"

Part of me wanted to say, "Hey! I have magic sneakers and I can run faster than any kid on earth!"

The other part of me knew my Zapato Power had to be a secret. How could I be a superhero if everyone knew where my power came from?

"I saw you forgot it, so I brought it for you," I said, handing the book over.

"Thanks!"

I know it's not the same as saving someone from a burning building, but it felt good to see Jason smile. And it felt good to know that I could run through the school, right past the principal, and all she would see was a puff of buzzing smoke.

My next chance to help someone came when we got back from the library. Maria remembered she'd left her lunch at home.

"I don't like meat loaf." She

crossed her arms and pouted. "Why did I forget my lunch on meat loaf day?"

I raised my hand like a rocket. "Can I go to the bathroom?"

Even though Mrs. Lane was pretty strict, she said yes. Ever since Justin had an accident, Mrs. Lane always said yes to the bathroom.

"Don't be long," she said. "We're leaving for lunch soon."

My feet buzzed with smoke the second I left the classroom.

ZOOM! ZOOM! ZAPATO!

I was back in Starwood Park, standing at Maria's front step, talking to Gio, Maria's little brother.

Gio is five. He only goes to kindergarten in the morning.

"See my puppy!" Gio said, holding it up for me to see. "I love my puppy."

He hugged a little black dog with cute white ears.

"Nice," I said. "What's its name?"

"Puppy," Gio said.

He walked away with the dog. I ran into Maria's house. Her mother was in the kitchen, but all she saw was a paper lunch bag disappear in a wisp of smoke.

ZOOM! ZOOM! ZaPaTO!

6. Poopee Isn't Good for Starwood Park

I should have been back at school with Maria's lunch in two seconds. But the toolshed made me stop. The door was open, and someone had written on the side in big red letters:

POOPEE

Mr. Vaslov had worked hard to paint the toolshed white. Now it had a big red bathroom word on it.

This wasn't good for Starwood Park.

I put down Maria's lunch and ran for some soap and water. In seconds, the shed was clean. But where was Maria's lunch? The paper bag was gone! I looked at my watch. It was time to wash hands and line up for the cafeteria. My chance to be a hero with Maria's lunch was over. I'd be lucky if I saved myself from Mrs. Lane. I closed the shed door.

ZOOM! ZOOM! ZAPATO!

I zipped back to school in a swirl of buzzing smoke.

"Why did you take so long in the bathroom?" Mrs. Lane asked when I walked into the room.

"I had a lot to do."

Mrs. Lane looked at me kind of funny, but that's all. Most teachers aren't brave enough to ask exactly what a kid did in the bathroom.

At lunch, Maria squished her meat loaf with her fork.

"What I need is super speed," she said. "Then I could run home.

Mama packed banana and jelly for me today."

Banana and jelly did not sound better to me than meat loaf, but I didn't tell Maria that. I also didn't tell her that super speed wouldn't help now that someone had stolen her lunch. Who would do that? And who wrote **POOPEE** on the toolshed? My head was full of questions, including who gave me my purple sneakers. Was Mom right? Did they come from one of my Dad's old friends?

All I knew was what I was going to do with my Zapato Power. I was going to stop whoever was trying to mess up Starwood Park.

At recess, my feet hummed like water rushing through pipes. From the playground, I can see my front door.

ZOOM! ZOOM! ZAPATO!

I was back home in half a blink, looking for answers. But I found more **POOPEE** than answers. This time someone had written **POOPEE** on the sidewalk.

I don't want Mom to see this, I thought. She'll think Starwood Park is turning into a bad neighborhood. We'll have to move again.

In a flash, I got more soap and water. The sidewalk was clean, but my brain was still dirty with questions. Who wrote POOPEE? Who stole Maria's lunch? And could Zapato Power help me solve both mysteries?

I looked behind the tool-shed. Nothing there except the yellow flowers Mr. Vaslov planted.

ZOOM! ZOOM! ZAPATO!

I ran around the building twice,

searching the walls and sidewalks for more red POOPEE. I didn't see any other bad words, but I did notice something else. The smoke coming from my sneakers covered me in a light cloud that made things sharper and clearer, like I was looking through a telescope. I could see every line between the bricks and the pattern of the curtains behind the windows.

If my purple sneakers came from one of Dad's soldier friends, they *could* be part of some kind of top secret army project. Could they do other stuff I didn't know about yet?

There wasn't time to stop and figure it all out. Mrs. Lane would be blowing the whistle to end recess soon.

I ran around the building a third
time, searching every blade of grass.
This time I got lucky. I found a

piece of red chalk. It was a good clue. Someone with red chalk wrote **POOPEE** on the shed and the sidewalk. Who? Could I figure it out if I kept running around? Or did I need something more than Zapato Power?

I checked my watch. Mrs. Lane would notice if I didn't come back from recess. She was the kind of teacher who counted heads to make sure no one was lost.

ZOOM! ZOOM! ZAPATO!

Even if Zapato Power couldn't solve all my mysteries, it could keep me out of trouble with Mrs. Lane.

7. Puppy Is Missing!

After school, Maria and I walked home together. Gio came running up with tears on his face.

"My puppy! She's missing!"

"Where did you see her last?" Maria asked.

"Over there." Gio pointed to the sidewalk. "I put down Puppy to write with chalk."

"Chalk?" I repeated, remembering my clue. "What word did you write?"

"My favorite word," Gio said. "I wrote 'Puppy.'"

That's when I solved my first mystery. Only it took more brain power than Zapato Power. Gio was the one who wrote **POOPEE** on the shed and sidewalk. He was a very bad speller.

"Puppy!" Gio cried again. "She ran away!"

"We have to find her," Maria said. "She could get hurt."

Puppy was too little to be alone. She could get run over by a car.

"Let's spread out and look in different places," I said.

Gio went right. Maria went left. I went everywhere.

ZOOM! ZOOM! ZAPATO!

I circled Starwood Park, my heels smoking, searching bushes, trees, and corners with my Zapato Power eyes.

ZOOM! ZOOM! ZAPATO!

I tried the school playground. I looked under the slides and all the benches, too. No little black dog with cute white ears.

ZOOM! ZOOM! ZAPATO!

I ran up and down the block, leaning down to check under parked cars. With my super speed, I had covered every inch for at least two miles. Puppy wasn't anywhere. By the time I met back up with Gio and Maria, I was worried.

"Do you think Puppy's been kidnapped?" I asked.

"No!" Gio started to cry again.

"Maybe Mr. Vaslov saw something," Maria suggested.

We walked over and knocked on the toolshed.

No one opened the door, but someone answered. "Ruff! Ruff!"

It was the second time in an hour that brain power worked better than Zapato Power. When were my purple sneakers going to make me a hero?

"Puppy!" Gio cried.

We pushed the door open. Inside on the floor was a pair of purple sneakers just like mine. Beside the sneakers was a little black dog with cute white ears chewing on a paper bag. Maria's lunch!

Just then, Mr. Vaslov walked up. "What's going on?"

Mr. Vaslov had a loud, deep voice. Maria, Gio, and I were used to it. But Puppy wasn't. She ran scared between his legs and out of the shed. We all chased after her as she raced toward the street. A blue car came around the corner.

"No!" Maria shouted.

Puppy was speeding. The blue car was speeding. Maria, Gio, and Mr. Vaslov couldn't keep up. But my purple sneakers could.

ZOOM! ZOOM! ZAPATO!

I dashed to the curb and scooped up Puppy before she ran into the street.

It was about time Zapato Power made me a hero.

Gio ran up to me. "Puppy! You saved her!"

"Ruff!" Puppy barked as she licked my face.

"She's saying thank you." Gio took the little black dog from my arms.

"No problem." I felt my cheeks spreading out in a huge smile. Then Maria and Mr. Vaslov joined us on the sidewalk.

"How did you do that?" Maria asked. "You were so fast you turned into a puff of smoke."

I gulped. What could I say that didn't sound too much like a lie? If I was going to use my Zapato Power a lot, I would need to learn how to talk as fast as I could run.

"Great job!" Mr. Vaslov patted my back. "Your feet were smoking, like an Olympic runner."

I stared at Mr. Vaslov. Was he saving me from Maria's question? I remembered the purple sneakers in the toolshed.

"Ruff!" Puppy barked again.

"Puppy wants to go home," Gio said, turning around.

We all walked back to Starwood Park. Gio and Maria went inside their apartment. I followed Mr. Vaslov. I had some questions for him.

8. I Solve the Final Mystery

"Mr. Vaslov?"

He was walking fast, like he didn't want me to catch up with him. Of course, he didn't get too far ahead. I had Zapato Power.

"Can I come inside your toolshed?"

Mr. Vaslov nodded his gray head and opened the door.

The purple sneakers were still on the floor beside Maria's chewed lunch bag. They had silver wings, just like mine, only they were lots bigger.

"Do you have super speed, too?" I asked Mr. Vaslov.

He sat down in a chair to put the sneakers on his feet. "I hope so."

"Let's race the train," I said.

We walked to the overhead track in the back of the building.

"I've watched you run here almost every day," Mr. Vaslov said. "Of all the boys I've seen come and go at Starwood Park, I knew you'd like my special sneakers the best."

Was Mr. Vaslov right about that?
Who wouldn't like running faster
than a train? But I didn't want to
argue with the man who gave me
Zapato Power.

"Thank you," I said.

Just then, we heard a train rumbling on the overhead track. Mr. Vaslov nodded at me.

"One, two, three!"

We both started racing. Only one of us reached the fence at the station. Me! Mr. Vaslov was way behind. I zipped back to where he was.

"Why don't your sneakers make you go as fast as me?"

Mr. Vaslov put his hand on his chest and caught his breath. "I'm not sure," he puffed. "I think it has something to do with weight. I can't make the physics work for someone my size."

"Then the purple sneakers only work for kids?"

"Right now." He took a handkerchief out of his pocket and wiped his face. "But I'm working on it."

So Mr. Vaslov was an inventor. I'd solved the last mystery, but another one was forming in my mind. What else could Mr. Vaslov invent?

"Can you make flying shoes?"

ZAPATO POWER